RETURN OF THE JEDI

Adapted by Geof Smith
Illustrated by Ron Cohee

 A GOLDEN BOOK • NEW YORK

© & ™ 2015 LUCASFILM LTD. All rights reserved. Published in the United States by Golden Books, an imprint of Random House Children's Books, a division of Penguin Random House LLC, 1745 Broadway, New York, NY 10019, and in Canada by Random House of Canada, a division of Penguin Random House Ltd., Toronto. Golden Books, A Golden Book, A Little Golden Book, the G colophon, and the distinctive gold spine are registered trademarks of Penguin Random House LLC.
randomhousekids.com
ISBN 978-0-7364-3548-2 (trade) — ISBN 978-0-7364-3549-9 (ebook)
Printed in the United States of America
10 9 8 7 6 5 4 3 2 1

A great war rages between the evil Galactic Empire and the Rebel Alliance. The Rebel hero **Han Solo** has been captured by the bounty hunter Boba Fett. Frozen in carbonite, Han is a trophy in the palace of the wormlike gangster **Jabba the Hutt**.

Luke Skywalker, the Jedi Knight, has a rescue plan. He sends R2-D2 and C-3PO to Jabba's lair on Tatooine as gifts.

A mysterious bounty hunter arrives to collect a reward for capturing Han's Wookiee copilot, **Chewbacca**.

The bounty hunter is really **Princess Leia**! Under cover of night, she frees Han from his icy prison. Unfortunately, Jabba's Gamorrean guards quickly **capture** them.

Soon after, Luke enters the palace and orders Jabba to release his friends. A **trapdoor** springs open. Jabba shakes with laughter as Luke falls into a dungeon! A mighty beast called a **rancor** attacks! Luke **crushes** it with a giant gate.

To punish Luke and his friends, Jabba will feed them to the **Sarlacc**, a sand monster. It will digest them for a thousand years!

But just before Luke is about to be eaten . . . he springs into action! R2-D2 tosses the Jedi his lightsaber. Throwing off his disguise, the Rebel **Lando Calrissian** joins the fight. The heroes quickly defeat Jabba and his henchmen.

KA-BOOM!

Han knocks Boba Fett into the Sarlacc pit. **BURP!** Luke and his friends escape Jabba's barge as it explodes.

Across the galaxy, Luke's father, **Darth Vader**, is about to set an evil plot in motion. He is overseeing construction of a new **Death Star**—a battle station so powerful it will be able to destroy the Rebels. A force shield generated on the nearby forest moon of Endor protects it. The Imperial Emperor tells Vader he wants Luke to join the Empire. "Together we can turn him to the **dark side** of the Force."

Luke flies his X-wing fighter to Dagobah to finish his Jedi training with **Yoda**. The wise old **Jedi Master** tells Luke he must confront Darth Vader. Just before Yoda fades away and becomes one with the Force, he whispers, "There is another Skywalker." Suddenly, the ghost of **Obi-Wan Kenobi**, Luke's first Jedi Master, appears. He reveals that Princess Leia is really Luke's sister!

Luke rejoins his friends on the Rebel convoy in space.
The commander of the Rebel fleet, Admiral Ackbar, has a
plan to **destroy** the new **Death Star**. Lando will lead
the space attack in the *Millennium Falcon*. Han, Luke, and
Leia will lead a strike team to the moon of Endor to disable
the force shield.

Soon Luke and his friends
land on Endor to complete their
mission. Scout troopers spot the
Rebels and **race away** on
speeder bikes to warn the Empire.

Luke and Leia hop onto a speeder bike and **chase** the scout troopers. The Rebels **zip** through the trees and quickly catch up.

Luke and Leia **stop** the Imperial scouts, but they become separated during the chase.

Lost, Leia meets a small, furry creature called an **Ewok**. His name is Wicket.

Luke rejoins Han and the Rebel strike team. They are worried because Leia has not returned. But as the heroes set off to find the princess, they are trapped in a net! **Whoosh!** The Rebels are **captured** by Ewoks!

Luke and Han are happy to find Leia safe and sound at the Ewoks' village. The creatures bow before **C-3PO**. They think he is **a golden god**! He tells the Ewoks stories of the Rebel Alliance's heroic struggles against the Empire. The Ewoks release Luke and his friends and agree to help **fight** the Imperial forces on their world.

At the controls of the *Millennium Falcon,* Lando and
his copilot, Nien Nunb, begin the Rebel **attack** on the
new Death Star. On Endor, Han's team and the Ewoks
prepare to destroy the shield generator.

The stormtroopers aren't prepared for enemies as small as the Ewoks. The Ewoks' simple **traps** made from logs and rocks overwhelm the Imperial walkers.

Han, Leia, and Chewbacca storm the bunker and disable the shield! Lando can now **destroy** the Death Star.

Luke **surrenders** to Darth Vader. He thinks there is still good in his father. But Vader delivers Luke to the Emperor on the Death Star. The Emperor wants Luke to unleash his rage and **join the dark side** of the Force. He makes the young Jedi fight Darth Vader!

Voosh!

Vader and Luke duel.

Klosh!

Luke wins the battle but refuses to finish off his father.

"If you will not be turned, you will be **destroyed**," the Emperor hisses. He shocks Luke with evil Force lightning from his fingers.

Zzzaap!

Darth Vader feels the **good** growing inside him. With the last of his strength, he rises up and **heaves** the Emperor into a deep reactor shaft!

The Death Star is about to be destroyed. Luke wants to **save** his father.

"No," Vader whispers. "You already have."

Meanwhile, the battle rages in space. Evading lasers and **zooming** TIE fighters, Lando and Nien Nunb fly the *Millennium Falcon* **deep** into the Death Star.

They destroy the main reactor, and the giant station begins to collapse. The Rebels speed away as the Death Star **explodes**!

The evil Empire is defeated! There is a **celebration** from Tatooine all the way to Endor.

The Ewoks sing and dance, and Chewbacca **roars**. R2-D2 beeps with joy.

Luke is happy the galaxy is safe—and the Force is at **peace** once again.